The Long-Lost Secret Diary of the World's Worst Dinosaur Hunter

First published in Great Britain by Scribo MMXVIII
Scribo, an imprint of
The Salariya Book Company
25 Marlborough Place, Brighton, BN1 1UB

ISBN 978-1-912233-19-9

The right of Tim Collins to be identified as the author of this work has
been asserted in accordance with sections 77 and 78 of the Copyright,
Designs and Patents Act, 1988.

Book design by David Salariya

© The Salariya Book Company
MMXVIII

Text copyright © Tim Collins

Series concept © The Salariya Book Company

Printed and bound in China

The text for this book is set in Century Schoolbook
The display type is Jacob Riley

www.salariya.com

Artwork credits
Illustrations: Sarah Horne
Additional cover illustrations: Liza Lewis

THE LONG-LOST SECRET DIARY OF THE WORLD'S WORST DINOSAUR HUNTER

Written by
Tim Collins

Illustrated by
Sarah Horne

SCRIBO
a SALARIYA *imprint*

Chapter I
—
Fossil Hunter

Wow! I wonder what this fossil is...

Monday February 28th, 1870

I found three fish lizard bones this morning, and I managed to get them to Father before the tourists arrived.

Every afternoon he waits for the coach from Bath to pull up at the inn and watches as the new visitors arrive in our village.

Then he races down to the lucky bone stall he keeps outside our house and writes his signs.

If he hears one of the tourists sneezing, he'll claim the bones can cure colds. If he sees one stooping, he'll claim they can cure bad backs. He once spotted a short, bad-tempered man and scribbled a sign that claimed the bones could make you taller and more agreeable, but the man just kicked his stall over.

Most of the time it works very well. Father's good at engaging the visitors in friendly conversation, and they're usually in high spirits at the start of their seaside holiday. By the time they realise the bones of my fish lizards are no more likely to cure their ailments than the bones they pick out of their Christmas goose, it's too late. Surprisingly few return to the stall and threaten to assault Father with the bones.

It's all very frustrating for me, however, because I know the bones are special. They're just not special in the way Father thinks.

I'm convinced they belonged to ancient creatures that lived in the sea in the very distant past. Father bought me some books and journals on the subject, and I discovered that learned men believe all manner of strange beasts walked the earth, swam in the oceans and flew in the air a very long time ago.

Not many remains of these creatures have been found yet, but every month brings new discoveries.

I believe my fish lizard bones belong to this new science. And I worry that my finds will end up on the mantelpieces of fickle tourists when they really ought to be studied by experts.

Whenever I explain this to Father, he says we make a good living from the bones, so it doesn't matter what they are.

*Tuesday March I*st

This proves I was right. Today Father sold some of my fish lizard bones for twenty pounds, which is a huge amount of money for us. And it wasn't because the man who bought them thought they'd cure his eyesight or back. It was because he knew what they were.

Father spotted a man with wild hair and a crumpled jacket stepping off the coach this afternoon. He rushed down to the stall and wrote a sign which made the unlikely claim that the fish lizard bones could cure untidiness. Surely carrying a dusty bone around would make someone look even more untidy?

The scruffy man soon took a stroll down from the inn to the seafront. Our house is on the main route, and Father was waiting behind his stall.

The man's jaw dropped when he saw the fish lizard bones. Father started his usual sales speech, but he didn't really need to. The man was turning the bones over in his hands one by one, and muttering in an excited fashion.

After a while he asked Father how much he wanted for all the bones on the table.

Father said he wouldn't take a penny less than five pounds, but the man offered twenty.

For once, Father was speechless. He prides himself on being good at haggling, but never before had he encountered a customer who offered to pay more, let alone four times the asking price. He sat frozen behind his stall as the man scooped up the bones and laid the banknotes out.

It was only when a breeze picked up and the money could have blown away that Father snapped out of his trance. He tucked the notes into his pocket and asked the man why he was so interested in the goods.

The man said he was a keen collector of ancient fossils and believed the bones were of great scientific interest.

Now maybe Father will listen to me when I tell him that the bones are worth more if we tell the truth about them.

GET REAL

The bones Ann has found belong to a large swimming reptile called Plesiosaur. It wasn't a dinosaur, though it lived at the same time as some of them. It had a broad, flat body with four flippers and a long neck. Many Plesiosaur skeletons were discovered in the early nineteenth century by the fossil hunter Mary Anning (see 'Hall of Fame' section).

Some people believe the legendary Loch Ness Monster is a Plesiosaur that survived extinction. But sadly for the Scottish tourist board, there is no evidence that such a creature exists.

Wednesday March 2nd

Father made me wait at home today in case the mysterious buyer called again. He thought the man might purchase even more bones if I was here too.

Sure enough, the man returned to our stall
in the middle of the morning. Father ushered
him in so I could tell him how I'd discovered
the fossils.

The man's name is William Armstrong and he
lives in London. He works as a surgeon, but
his real passion is collecting bones. He said the
remains I'd gathered were some of the finest
he'd ever seen and he intended to show them
at the next meeting of the Geological Society
in London.

It's usually embarrassing when visitors come to
our house. Every inch is filled with the bones I
gather from the beach, and most people are put
off. We once invited a vicar from Bath inside for
tea, and he fainted when a grinning fish lizard
skull slid down into his lap. Father lay him
on my collection of fossilised fish lizard poo to
recover, but this only distressed him more.

It was a different matter with Mr Armstrong. Not only did he love my bone collection, but he was very impressed with the fossilised poo too. He said the Geological Society would love to hear about it.

Mr Armstrong questioned me about the bones at great length. Whenever I spoke, Father butted in to point out the excellent quality of the specimens, which wasn't helpful. I was trying to have a serious conversation with a fellow scientist, and all he could do was interrupt with his sales talk.

At one point, Mr Armstrong stood up and clapped his hands together. He said he'd had a brilliant idea. He would pay for Father and me to come to London so I could present the findings to the Geological Society myself.

I wanted to do this more than anything else in the world, but I found myself unable to speak. I could only stare at Mr Armstrong and nod. I hope I manage to say more in front of the Society.

Now Mr Armstrong is making arrangements for Father and me to come to London with him. I can't believe I'm going to such a huge city. I've never been further than Bath before, and even that seemed impossibly busy. London is many, many times bigger.

Thursday March 3rd

I think my luck is changing at last. All my life I've wanted to be a great scientist, but I feel like I've been under a foul curse. Whenever a chance of success has come along, fate has worked against me.

A great scientist from London called William Pringles once stayed at the local inn. When I discovered he was there, I gathered a selection of my best bone fragments and went up to show him. I was sure he'd be so impressed he'd tell all the other scientists in London about them and I would finally get some recognition.

I spotted him eating soup at one of the tables and hurried over. Unfortunately, I tripped as I approached and the bones sploshed right into his bowl. If they'd landed just a few inches to the side, I might still have been able to tell him about my fish lizards. As it was, he was so furious about the filthy scraps of bone in his onion and potato soup, he wouldn't have cared if I'd discovered the secrets of alchemy. He refused to listen to my apologies and demanded I leave immediately.

I'd come to accept that setbacks like this would always happen to me. Yet now I am just days away from sharing my finds with London's finest experts. Maybe things are finally turning around.

Friday March 4th

There was a huge storm last night, which always makes for excellent bone-harvesting. The waves lash against the cliffs, sending new rocks tumbling down to the beach. I tap them apart with my hammer and search for remains inside. When I find some, I set about the slow process of removing them without damaging them.

I was so busy with my work I didn't spot Mr Armstrong approaching, and he gave me quite a fright when he nudged me on the shoulder.

I advised him to return to the town. It can be very dangerous around the cliffs. The ground is slippery, rocks can crash down onto your head, and the tide sweeps in so quickly you could be stranded if you didn't know exactly when to leave.

But Mr Armstrong insisted on staying. As I worked, he told me how the huge swimming lizards ended up buried in rocks. He said the whole area was covered in water many years ago, and when the fish lizards died they sunk to the bottom of the sea. Eventually, the climate changed and the bones were covered in mud and sand that hardened into rock.

I'd worked much of this out from the journals, but I'd never had it explained so simply before. The scientists in the journals use very complicated words, and it's hard to follow what they mean.

As he watched me extract a rib, Mr Armstrong said I was one of the best fossil hunters he'd ever seen, and that I should travel the country and search for other discoveries to go with my fish lizards.

I told him I couldn't afford it, but he said some of the men from the Geological Society are very rich and might sponsor me if they like my talk. They may be a little strange and stuffy, but if I got them onside it might help my career.

Hearing Mr Armstrong talk about my 'career' made me truly believe I had shaken off my bad luck at last. But what he said next went beyond even my ambitions.

He clapped his hands together, and said he'd had a better idea. He pointed to the mist-shrouded ocean and said I should go there. At first I thought he was suggesting I hunt for fossils in the sea. I thought this was a terrible idea, as I would be unable to breathe.

It turned out he was actually suggesting I cross the sea in a huge ship and visit the New World. He's done a lot of research into the landscape of the Western United States of America, and he believes many ancient creatures are buried there.

These would be the huge lizards that walked on the land, rather than the ones that swam in the sea. The men in the Society call them 'dinosaurs', which means 'terrible lizards'. Only a few have been found so far, but Mr Armstrong thinks I could find a great deal more in America.

He said he wants to do it himself, but he can't take the time off work. He thinks some of the really wealthy members of the Society might pay for Father and me to go if I impress them.

I was already a little overwhelmed by the idea of visiting London. The thought of crossing the sea to the New World makes me feel dizzy. But Mr Armstrong seems to think it's not just possible, but probable.

He has an odd talent for making you believe the most unlikely of things will happen. Out there on the beach, I really believed I could sail around the world and hunt dinosaurs.

Now I'm back in my room updating my journal, it all seems like a silly fancy. I've only ever travelled a few miles from my front door before. I am not qualified to explore the globe, and if I ever tried, my bad luck would ensure the whole thing ended in disaster.

Saturday March 5th

Mr Armstrong went hiking along the coast today, so I was left alone on the beach. I searched around the rocks, but I couldn't concentrate. I kept putting my hammer down and staring at the sea.

Could I really cross it? The more I thought about it, the more possible it seemed.

If one of the rich men in the Society wants to pay for me to go to America, why shouldn't I?

I fancied I could see the New World across the ocean, and that the huge lizards were standing on the shore and beckoning me.

I've made my mind up. If one of the wealthy geologists wants to pay for me to travel to the New World, I'll do it.

GET REAL

The term 'dinosaur' was coined by the scientist Sir Richard Owen. It comes from Greek words meaning 'terrible' and 'lizard'. He meant 'terrible' in the sense of 'awe-inspiring' rather than 'really scary' or 'rubbish'. Dinosaurs aren't really lizards at all. And if they tried to pass themselves off as lizards they'd be terrible at it, so the name is really quite accurate if you think about it.

Sunday March 6th

A few food barrels washed up on the beach this morning, so I hid them behind a rock and went up to tell the Joss the innkeeper about them. He's meant to report them to the local customs men, who seize them on behalf of the government, but what he really does is smash them open to share with the people of the village.

Father and I are lucky. Between my bone-harvesting skills and his selling skills, we earn more than enough to live. But most people in the village are poor, and some go for days without food. So if a few barrels wash up on the shore from a wrecked ship, it only seems fair that I should let Joss know.

The only drawback is that I have to tell him about the fish lizard bones every time, and he still seems very confused by them.

'Still digging those dead lizards out of the rocks?' asked Joss as I led him to the seafront.

'Yes,' I said. 'And I'm going to London on Friday to talk to the Geological Society about them.'

'Bad place, London,' he muttered.

He stared up at the cliff as we approached.

'If you ask me, those lizards shouldn't have crawled up there in the first place,' he said. 'It's no wonder they died.'

'I don't think it happened like that,' I said. 'I think they died first, then the rocks sort of built up on top of them.'

Mr Armstrong had made it all sound so simple, but Joss was screwing his face up in confusion now.

'All this land used to be covered in water,' I said. 'Even the cliffs.'

'Nah,' said Joss. 'Old Will has never mentioned anything about water on the rocks and he remembers everything.'

'This is before even he was born,' I said. 'A very long time before, in fact.'

'I still say the lizards should have kept out of them rocks,' he said, shaking his head. 'They were asking for trouble.'

I hope I do a better job of explaining myself to the Society next week. But I expect it's easier to discuss such things with learned men. Joss gets all his information from what the other villagers tell him, which is why he refuses to yawn in case his spirit escapes through his mouth and the devil jumps in.

Chapter 2

⊢—⊣

Journey to London

Monday March 7ᵗʰ

How will we fit on the coach with all these
cases? I need all the bones and fossilised poo I
can carry for my presentation, but there's no
need for Father to bring three full trunks too.
He says he wants to bring plenty of fish lizard
bones to sell to rich Londoners, but I think he
ought to be careful.

Joss isn't correct about much, but he was right
to say that London can be a dangerous place.
The hardened locals might not be forgiving if
Father singles them out for having bad skin or
poor posture.

Tuesday March 8ᵗʰ

Much as I suspected, we made ourselves very
unpopular with the other passengers by lugging
all our cases on. Father made things even worse
by opening one of his and trying to sell a bone

to the grumpy woman opposite on the grounds that it could cure her 'sullen and pinched expression'. His silence would have been a better cure for her bad temper.

We are now staying in a hotel near Bath railway station. I can see a huge plume of smoke rising into the air every time a train chugs past. It's all very exciting, but I must try

and sleep. I'll be getting onto one of those things for the first time tomorrow, and I want to be well rested for it.

Wednesday March 9ᵗʰ

When I woke up this morning, I thought my bad luck had returned. The cases of bones I'd left at the foot of the bed had gone, and Father was nowhere to be seen. My mind raced through all the cruel tricks fate could have played. I imagined that the bones had been stolen by local thieves, that Father had chased after them in vain, and that I would have to face the Geological Society with no evidence of my finds.

I raced outside to see Father instructing some boys from the hotel to carry the bones over to the station. Everything was fine. The crisis had all been in my mind, and my curse had not struck.

We soon boarded the train, which turned out to be much more pleasant than the coach. Our carriage was almost empty so we could pile all our luggage in without upsetting anyone. Mr Armstrong was kind enough to pay for us to travel in a first-class carriage. It would have been cheaper in a third-class carriage, but it would have been much more cramped and we might not have been able to sit at all.

I stared out of the large window and watched the countryside speed past. It soon made me dizzy, so I closed my eyes, and before long I found myself drifting off. I can't believe I spent all that time looking forward to my first train journey, and when it finally arrived I slept through it.

When I woke up we'd arrived at Paddington Station, which was filled with steam and smoke and mad rushing crowds. Mr Armstrong said we could take a train that went under the ground, but the idea frightened Father, who got it into his head that the vehicle would burrow into the soil like a mole, rather than travel along a tunnel.

We couldn't find a cab, so we lugged our bags down the street instead. Mr Armstrong led us along a wide road that was bustling with carts, carriages and omnibuses. At one point I had to leap aside from a strange pedal bicycle with a huge wheel on the front and a small wheel on the back.

Father suggested buying one to take back home, but I don't think it would be much use on our steep hill. It would be good for a rapid one-way trip into the sea, but that's about all.

London is just as exciting as I hoped, but I was struck by the smell. There's a stink like rotten vegetables everywhere. And at night a thick yellow fog descends, making everything dismal and dreary.

Thank heavens we are staying in the rooms Mr Armstrong keeps above his practice. Arriving in the city would have been much more frightening if we'd had to find somewhere to board.

Mr Armstrong's small, hunched housekeeper Mrs Baker made us feel very welcome with a light supper, though her mood soured when she realised our cases were full of fossils.

'He should worry about the bones of his patients, not them horrid lizards,' she muttered. 'They're not going to put food on the table.'

'They would if he told everyone about their fantastic properties,' said Father. He plucked one of the bones out of his case. 'This one can aid with posture, for example. It's yours for just sixpence, and I'm cutting my own throat at that price.'

Mrs Baker looked like she'd happily cut his throat for him. How inappropriate of Father to switch into sales mode when Mr Armstrong is giving us free food and board. He needs to pick his moments more wisely.

GET REAL

The arrival of the railways transformed Victorian Britain. Engineers such as Isambard Kingdom Brunel oversaw vast networks that were built at amazing speed. By 1870, the rail network covered over 20,000 kilometres. Even people without much money could use the trains, with third-class tickets costing as little as a penny a mile. But travelling conditions were cramped and uncomfortable.

Thursday March 10th

Mr Armstrong let me work in his library today. He has hundreds of books and journals about dinosaurs and ancient beasts.

Father could find nothing to interest him, so he announced he was going out for a stroll. I warned him to watch out for rogues and villains, but he told me he was perfectly capable of looking after himself.

He arrived back two hours later and announced that I'd been fussing about nothing, and most of the Londoners he'd met were perfectly charming. He said that a young man had accidentally knocked him over at one point, but he had taken great pains to help him up and pat the dirt off his coat.

I asked Father what time it was, but when he reached into his pocket he found his watch was missing. It had disappeared from the exact place the 'friendly' young man had patted.

Father flushed red as he worked out what had happened. I hope he'll be more cautious from now on.

This evening Mr Armstrong took me through his maps of the American West and marked out the places he thought the best 'bone beds' would be. These are places rich with fossils, which should provide excellent hunting ground for dinosaurs.

There are seven sites in walking distance from railway stops. From East to West, they are:

Creston Rock
Rolling Valley
Hell Creek
Black Canyon
Midway
Rock Spring
Pine Bluff

Tomorrow Mr Armstrong will consult his travel agent and see if he can work up a schedule that takes me through these stops, with a week of field work at each.

We might be going too far with this planning, as the trip is still only a dim possibility. But if any of the rich men from the Society want to sponsor me, I'll be able to tell them exactly where I want to go and how much it will cost, which will make things much simpler.

Friday March 11ᵗʰ

Tomorrow is the big day. I'll be addressing
the Society at five. I prepared my talk in Mr
Armstrong's library today, and I hoped Father
might be able to stay there and keep out
of trouble.

My hope proved unfounded. Shortly after lunch,
he announced he was going out to sell the bones.
I was too distracted by my preparation to argue
with him, so I let him go.

He arrived back two hours later looking rather
shaken. After wandering for a few minutes, he'd
managed to find an empty stall in a market and
he'd laid the bones on top of it.

There were too many people to tailor individual
signs for, so he just wrote:

Miracle Bones - Ask for Details

A very large man walked past and father claimed that the bones could banish unsightly jowls. The man took exception and attempted to assault father with one of the bones.

Meanwhile, the owner of a stall selling miracle tonic water stormed over and accused Father of stealing his custom. The large man accidentally hit this stall owner, and a scuffle broke out. A horse bolted, spilling the fruit and vegetables from its cart. Thieves descended on the scene, and by the time things had calmed down all the fruit, vegetables and bones had gone.

A police officer soon turned up, but when Father told him his collection of giant lizards had been stolen, he dismissed him as insane and moved on to the next witness.

I told Father he'd end up in trouble. Maybe now he'll learn to be careful in London.

It's the fish lizards I feel sorry for. These magnificent beasts deserve better than to end up on the black market, being sold in dark alleyways by scoundrels.

Mr Armstrong's travel agent has drawn up a schedule for my New World dinosaur hunt, sailing from Bristol to New York in July, heading west by train to reach the bone beds in August and September, then sailing back in October.

It's all beginning to feel frighteningly real, but I mustn't get my hopes up just yet. First I need to impress the men from the Society. The richest three are called Sir Fitzhugh Xavier Sapping, Sir Hobart Remmington Risewell and Sir Leopold Pinkerton Hamilton. Mr Armstrong is convinced my trip will be funded if I impress at least one of them.

Saturday March 12th

We arrived at the Geological Society late this afternoon. Mr Armstrong left me in the hall to set up my fish lizard bones while he ushered the members in.

The first were three scowling men with grey hair who all looked as though they were trying to digest raw potatoes. They sat on the front seats and glared at me, the first cupping his hand to his ear, the second adjusting his thick eyeglasses and the third smoothing down the wild tufts of hair on either side of his head.

It shouldn't have surprised me that the most esteemed geologists in the country should be so ancient, but these three looked like they'd have been alive when the fish lizards were still swimming around.

When the hall was full, I began my speech.
The man with the thick eyeglasses let out loud
grunts after everything I said, and I couldn't
work out if he was angry or clearing his throat.

After I'd talked about each of the bones, I
laid them out on the floor to reconstruct a full
skeleton. There was a great commotion as the
geologists shuffled forward to look.

The elderly man with the mad tufts of hair
spoke first. 'Stuff and nonsense,' he said. 'A
little girl like you couldn't find a genuine
prehistoric creature. I've no doubt it's simply a
crocodile that got lost.'

'They could be the bones of a tall human,'
said the man cupping his ear. 'My nephew saw
a chap who was nine feet tall once.'

'Or a dog,' said the man with the thick glasses. 'I saw one as big as a horse in the park the other day.'

'Were you wearing your glasses?' I asked.

'Don't be ridiculous,' said the man. 'I leave them at home to go to the park.'

'Well, how do you know it wasn't a horse?' I asked.

An angry murmur swept through the room.

'Dashed impertinence!' shouted a man from the back. 'Are you telling Sir Leopold Pinkerton Hamilton that he doesn't know the difference between a dog and a horse?'

I felt my heart sink. Sir Leopold Pinkerton Hamilton was one of the rich men Mr Armstrong

had told me to impress. It didn't look like he'd be sponsoring me, then.

'I'm sorry,' I said. 'I didn't mean to speak out of turn. But I'm convinced these are the remains of a huge lizard that swam in the sea, not a tall man or a big dog or a lost crocodile. The remains of many such ancient creatures have been found. So why shouldn't this also be one?'

'Because they were discovered by men of science,' said the man with the eyeglasses. 'They weren't just fancies dug from a schoolgirl's sandpit.'

I felt my cheeks heating and found myself scrunching my fists into balls. If these were really scientists, why weren't they considering the evidence before them? They were blinded to the importance of my finds by my age and sex.

Mr Armstrong leapt to his feet and clapped his hands. The chatter stopped.

'Gentlemen, let's save our comments for the end,' he said. 'I'll be happy to present my account of the evidence if Miss Mansfield's words are unclear.'

I decided to move on to my next topic, which was fossilised poo. This was meant to be the centrepiece of my speech, as Mr Armstrong had told me that no one had ever discussed it with the Society before. When I'd planned my speech, I was imagining it as a breakthrough moment, with everyone standing and applauding. But now I wasn't feeling so confident.

I held up a poo fossil.

'I often find rocks like this near fish lizard bones,' I said. 'I began to wonder why, and careful examination led me to believe these are not really rocks at all, but the fossilised poo of the fish lizard creatures.'

The geologists pulled disgusted faces, as if I'd suggested they eat the dung rather than merely look at it.

'I believe that by studying it, we can learn about the diet of the creatures,' I said.

The man with the mad tufts of hair rose to his feet.

'That's quite enough,' he shouted. 'These topics might raise a smile among your school friends, but I can assure you they are not appropriate in this company.'

I ran over and shoved the fossil towards him so he could examine it for himself. He couldn't have looked more horrified if it had been fresh.

The man stormed out, muttering angrily. One by one, the others followed, until finally there was just Father and Mr Armstrong left.

My chance to visit the New World has surely gone now. It seems I have not managed to escape my curse after all.

GET REAL

Fossilised pieces of poo can give us important information about extinct species, such as whether they ate plants or animals. The fossil-hunter Mary Anning noticed that dark grey pebbles were often found near the skeletons of marine lizards. She found that these stones contained small fish bones when broken apart, and wondered if they were lumps of ancient dung. She shared her findings with the geologist William Buckland, who coined the term 'coprolites' for them.

Sunday March 13th

According to Mr Armstrong, the two men on either side of Sir Leopold Pinkerton Hamilton were Sir Fitzhugh Xavier Sapping and Sir Hobart Remmington Risewell, which makes me feel a little better. The three men who could have paid for my trip were against me from the moment they saw me. They would never have sponsored me, no matter how well my presentation went.

Mr Armstrong said they might warm to me over time. When he first attended meetings of the Society, he presented his collection of dinosaur back vertebrae. Sir Leopold Pinkerton Hamilton insisted they were the teeth of a huge dog and the others agreed. But the following week he returned with some actual dog teeth to show them the difference and he won them round.

I don't think they'll ever change their minds
about me. Not unless I return with the greatest
set of fossils they've ever seen. But I'd need
to go to America for those, and I can't do that
without one of them sponsoring me.

It's no use. I'll just go home and look for more
fish lizard bones. The tourists like them, even if
the scientists don't.

Monday March 14th

We're going back tomorrow, but Mr Armstrong
has one final idea to save my American trip.
I'm going to write to universities here and in
America, outlining my discoveries and asking
for funding. I'll enclose my schedule and a full
outline of the costs.

Mr Armstrong seems hopeful, and he's lending
me a huge collection of journals and maps to

take home, so I'll be prepared if I ever make it to America. But I know my luck too well to believe it will ever happen.

Thursday March 17th

We're home now. I returned to the seafront today and hunted for fossils.

I wish I could bring Sir Leopold Pinkerton Hamilton, Sir Fitzhugh Xavier Sapping and Sir Hobart Remmington Risewell to the beach. I'd show them how I find the bones and how I separate them from the clay and sandstone. Then they'd have to believe that my finds are genuine. And if they didn't I could leave them stranded on the rocks while the tide rushed in.

Chapter 3

Going West

Monday March 21st

I had my first reply from one of the universities today. It's from Boniface College, Cambridge, but it's not much help.

Dear Miss Mansfield

I'm afraid I cannot offer any aid for your expedition to the New World, and indeed I would advise you to abandon it.

It is my belief that all living things over there are inferior to those here. Their repulsive land is littered with gloomy swamps, dingy forests and dry deserts. As a consequence, all their native beasts are small and feeble compared to our noble steeds, proud bulldogs and honest badgers. You would do better to roll your sleeves up and dig in the English soil for British fossils that will be the pride of our empire and the envy of our foes!

Yours sincerely

Professor Welton Stanway Kibble

GET REAL

Amazingly, some scientists really did believe that native animals in the 'new world' of America would be inferior to those in the 'old world' of Europe. The idea came from the French naturalist Comte de Buffon, who lived in the eighteenth century. His ideas angered Thomas Jefferson so much that he ordered his soldiers to catch a huge moose to prove him wrong.

Wednesday March 23rd

I got another reply to my request today, this time from Saint Stephen's College, Oxford. It wasn't any more promising.

Dear Miss Mansfield

I'm afraid I can't offer you financial aid for your expedition, but I do have a favour to ask. I'm currently engaged in a wager with Professor Jacob Bilton Meredith to see who can eat the widest variety of living creatures. Just this week I have enjoyed a guinea pig pie, a hedgehog tart and a sea slug trifle. I would be most grateful if you could bring back the following ingredients from the New World:

A bison
A coyote
An opossum

Cure the meat if it looks like it's spoiling in the heat. But don't worry too much, I have an excellent stomach.

I can't wait to see the look on old Meredith's face when I serve up that little lot in a crumble!

Yours sincerely

Professor Ignacio Baldry Fitzsimons

P.S. I strongly recommend bread and weasel pudding.

I have no intention of honouring this bizarre request. I have no idea how oddballs like Professor Baldry Fitzsimons and Professor Stanway Kibble get such important posts, while honest men like Mr Armstrong have to pay for their own field work and receive very little recognition. I wonder if all science is as unfair as this, or just fossil-hunting?

GET REAL

Some of the most famous dinosaur hunters were very odd characters. The geologist William Buckland attempted to eat his way through the entire animal kingdom, and is known to have served his guests mice on toast and roast hedgehog. He thought the most disgusting creatures of all were moles and bluebottles, so avoid those next time you're in the supermarket.

*Thursday April 28*th

No more replies from university professors.
Even another weird one would be better than
nothing.

I'll just have to accept that my dream of visiting
America and becoming a great scientist is over.

I can now see that my curse was following
me all along. It was simply allowing me a few
moments of hope to make things all the more
bitter when it struck again.

No doubt I shall be stuck on this beach
forever, digging out ancient bones for
ungrateful tourists.

*Friday April 29*th

This morning I told Father I didn't feel like
collecting any new fossils. I thought this might

make him angry. He's been working very hard on his stall recently, and I've had to collect a lot of bones to replace the ones he's sold. But instead of frowning, he rooted around in a pile of rocks in the corner.

'I hoped some of those professors would come up with the money,' he said. 'But I thought of a back-up plan in case they didn't.'

He dragged out a wooden chest and opened it to reveal a huge stash of sovereigns and crowns.

'We can't use that,' I said. 'That's everything you've ever earned from the stall.'

'You earned it too,' he said. 'It wouldn't have been much of a bone stall with no bones. If you've got your heart set on the New World, let's go. I'm keen to see what all the fuss is about myself.'

I tried arguing, but Father wouldn't hear a word.

So it seems we are going to America after all. Can I really have escaped my curse at last?

I can't wait to get out there and hunt some dinosaurs. But there is so much to arrange first. I'll start by writing to Mr Armstrong, so he can get his travel agent to book everything. Then I need to work out what to bring, and study the maps and journals over and over again. I expect this shall be my last diary entry for some while.

*Monday July II*th

I am writing this from the saloon of our steamship *The City of Bristol*. We set off at seven this morning. One of the crewmen fired a gun and the huge vessel crept away from the dock. The passengers crowded onto the deck to wave handkerchiefs at their friends and family.

Soon we were leaving Bristol far behind and the mood became more sombre. I noticed a few women lifting their handkerchiefs to their eyes to brush away tears. No doubt they were missing the loved ones they'd left behind. Even Father was subdued, which is very unusual. I wonder if all the sad partings reminded him of when we lost Mother. I'd rather not dwell on such things, so I didn't ask him.

Already we are far out at sea, and my heart races every time we roll over a large wave. I know our ship's safety equipment is excellent, and we're in no real danger, but it feels very strange to be listing about so violently with nothing but water for miles around.

Tuesday July 12th

I was worried Father would get bored and I'd have to keep him entertained, but luckily he's made friends with some gentlemen from Boston, leaving me free to study my maps and journals.

He must be getting on well with the Boston men, as he seems in very good spirits whenever I run into him.

Wednesday July 13th

Father is no longer friends with the gentlemen from Boston, as they caught him cheating at cards. I should have known from his wide grin that he was up to something.

Father claimed it was all just a practical joke and that he was planning to give their money back at the end of the journey, but it didn't stop

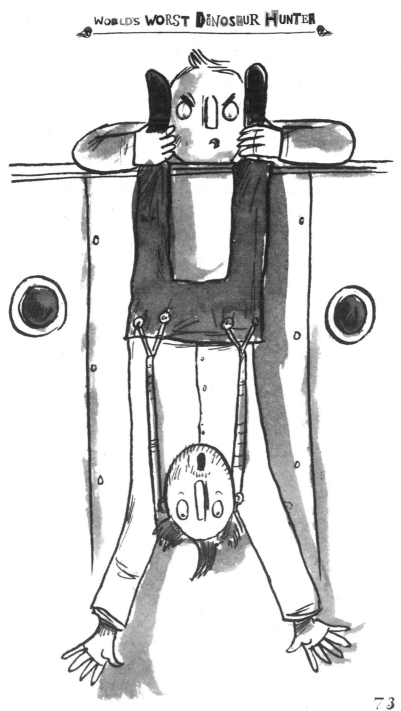

them dangling him over the side of the ship and making him promise to stay away from them for the rest of the journey.

All of which means I've got to find ways to keep him occupied for the next week. Right now I've got him copying out a list of currently known dinosaurs from Mr Armstrong's journals. I've already done this myself, but I'm pretending it's vital for our trip to keep him out of trouble.

Thursday July 14th

When I woke up this morning I found our cabin swaying violently. I became convinced that my bad luck was following us across the sea and that a great storm would sink us before we even reached the New World. But when I stepped out onto the deck I saw a crewman strolling along and whistling with his hands in his pockets. He seemed very confused when I asked him what

was wrong. Apparently our crossing is very calm, and there's nothing to worry about. It certainly doesn't feel that way.

Friday July 15th

The ship began to lurch about again this afternoon. We were sitting in the saloon, and a great many of the ladies and gentlemen around us had to rush out to vomit over the side. Father and I were very amused to watch all the refined folk breaking off their sophisticated conversations to spew. Or at least we were until our own stomachs gave out and we had to join them.

The noise was quite deafening. The crew wouldn't have needed to sound the steam whistle if another ship had approached. The sound of us all retching must have rung out for miles.

Wednesday July 20ᵗʰ

We are now heading into the port of New
York, a mere nine days after we left Bristol.
We've been following the coast for the last two
days, which I found rather surprising. New
York isn't the closest point to England, but
it's the most important, so this is where we're
heading. It must be frustrating for the people of
Massachusetts or Maine to watch their towns

sail by, knowing they have a long rail journey ahead when they reach New York.

The sun is very powerful now. I've ventured out onto deck to get myself used to the heat, but I can't stay out long without feeling faint.

I must persevere. The heat in the West will be much fiercer.

Thursday July 21ˢᵗ

I am writing this from our hotel in New York. We made it all the way here without any deadly storms, icebergs or sea monsters. I hardly dare say it, but I believe I have left my curse back at home. Perhaps it was afraid to cross the water.

New York is just as crowded and dirty as London, and the smell is even worse because of the heat.

We had to lug our trunk for half an hour to find our hotel. Everywhere was packed with people in a desperate hurry, and most were annoyed with us for going slowly.

As well as American accents, I heard Irish and Scottish voices and some European languages that Father said were Italian and German. People are coming from all over the world to this huge city. I wonder where everyone will live if it keeps growing at this rate?

I don't think Father really understands how big this city is. He keeps introducing himself to people and telling them he'll see them around. I explained that there are almost a million people here. The chance of meeting any of them again is tiny.

Friday July 22nd

I was wrong. Father did indeed run into someone again. It was a woman in a green dress he'd spoken to outside our hotel last night. He spotted her this morning and greeted her like an old friend. She clearly didn't remember him, because she shrieked and ran away down the street. This sent Father into a long rant about how New Yorkers are unfriendly. I explained that they see lots of people every day. You can't expect them to remember everyone.

Father finally snapped out of his foul mood when he spotted a small group playing cards around a crate. He was desperate to join in, but I convinced him to hold back and observe them. I'm glad I did as the whole thing turned out to be a confidence trick.

It was called 'Three Card Monte' and you had to follow the Queen of Hearts as the dealer rearranged a row of three cards. It cost a nickel to play, but if you got it right you got your nickel back, plus an extra one. At first there seemed to be many winners, but I soon worked out that anyone who took money from the dealer was secretly a friend of his. Whenever a genuine member of the public played, they lost. The dealer skilfully laid out the cards to make sure they always chose the wrong one. He did it so fast you could barely see it, but you could tell what he was doing if you concentrated on his hands.

Father was very impressed when I explained the scam to him and he said he'll try it on the tourists when we get home. I don't think this is a good idea. It's one thing to trick people in a huge city where you can disappear into the crowd. It's another to do it in a tiny village with nowhere to hide and plenty of tall cliffs to throw you off.

Saturday July 23rd

Our long railroad journey west begins today.
It will take us over two weeks just to get to
the first bone bed, Creston Rock. It just goes
to show what a vast country this is. You can
travel at high speed for weeks and still not
reach the end.

After trying to make friends with hundreds
of locals, Father finally found someone who
wanted to talk to him today. He wandered
down the platform as we were waiting for the
train, and found a man with a white moustache
who was happy to hear all about our trip. I
was hoping he might get on our train and
keep Father occupied, but he was waiting for
a different one. At least Father's changed his
mind about all New Yorkers being rude, even if
it did happen right at the end of our stay.

Since we boarded the train, Father's been
trying to teach himself to deal cards like the con
artist. This should take him hours to master,
which will give me plenty of time to study my
maps and journals.

Monday August 1ˢᵗ

We're passing into dry, mysterious territory. I
feel as though the ancient lizards are calling
me from their graves in the hot ground. None
of those stuffy old fools from the Society would
dare come this far west. There are lawless
bandits and violent locals out here. Even if the
great lizards came back to life, they wouldn't be
the most dangerous thing around.

Let the cowards back home argue over their
tiny scraps of backbone. I'm striking out to
gather some real fossils.

Wednesday August 3ʳᵈ

The heat is becoming unbearable. I have been
cooling myself with my fan all day, and my
arms are so tired I can hardly write.

If the train is speeding along its tracks, air rushes in and cools us, but when it stops, sweat drips down my face.

It is difficult enough to put up with the temperature while relaxing in a carriage. I can only imagine how tough it must have been for the workers who built this railroad.

We are staying in a boarding house by the side of the station tonight. Most of the other travellers who have ventured this far west are young men working on the railroads and in the mines. It's almost midnight and they're still making a deafening noise in the saloon next door. They seem to switch between fearsome arguments and rowdy songs.

Father has now perfected his card dealing and he wanted to try it out on them, but I persuaded him to stay. Some of them are carrying revolvers, and if he tried the Three Card Monte trick on any of them, it would be the last thing he ever did.

GET REAL

The first transcontinental railroad was completed in 1869. Within just a few years, it had transformed the USA. It became much easier for people to travel west to farm the land, and industries such as mining boomed. But it was bad news for the American Buffalo. Professional hunters moved west and almost drove the species to extinction.

Chapter 4

Digging for Bones

Thursday August 11ᵗʰ

We have finally arrived at our first bone bed.
This evening we got off the train at Creston
Rock, and checked into the local boarding
house. Early tomorrow we shall venture out to
the place Mr Armstrong marked on the map.
The heat is so intense in the middle of the day
that we'll only be able to work in the morning
and the evening. But if the ground around here
is as rich with fossils as Mr Armstrong seemed
to believe, we should strike gold before long.

Friday August 12ᵗʰ

Nothing so far. We walked for half an hour
until we came to the place Mr Armstrong had
marked. It was a stretch of flat, dry land at the
base of a rocky ridge that ran from east to west.

According to Mr Armstrong, the ground should
have been full of fossils. But there was no sign

of any by the time Father had dug six feet into the earth. By then the heat was rising and we had to return.

This evening we tried a place several feet away, but it also yielded nothing. But this was just the first day. We have five more before we must move on to our next stop.

Monday August 15th

Four days have gone by and still we've found no bones. We've tried digging at intervals of ten feet all along the ridge, but with no success.

Father got so frustrated he insisted on digging until after noon, when we should have been resting in the shade of our room. When even this extra effort produced nothing, he collapsed onto the rocky ground.

He said he didn't mind if we found nothing, because we've both had a wonderful holiday. It didn't sound very convincing as he lay there gasping for breath, with his sweat running into the dust.

We came here to find dinosaurs, not to enjoy the scenery. We shall have to keep trying.

Thursday August 18th

I'm writing this from the station. We are sitting on empty cases and waiting to go to the next stop on our schedule, Rolling Valley. No one else is here except two railroad workers to our right and a solitary man at the far end of the platform.

Father and I have said nothing this morning. But I expect he's wondering the same thing. What if Mr Armstrong was wrong? What if there are no bones in the places he marked? What if the ancient beasts never lived here at all?

It means we'll have spent all our savings and sacrificed half a year for nothing. So much for leaving my bad luck back at home. It has followed me all the way here, just as it will follow me to the grave.

No. I mustn't think like this. I shall keep going and discover some amazing bones and I shall become known as the greatest fossil hunter in the world.

Friday August 19th

Wonderful news! We have found something at last! We strolled out of our new boarding house as the sun rose and made for the second place Mr Armstrong had marked. Within an hour we had struck our first bone, which was a tiny tail vertebra. It wasn't very grand, but it was intact.

I found three more this afternoon, and I reconstructed part of the beast's tail on my bed this evening.

It isn't going to throw Sir Leopold Pinkerton Hamilton and his friends into a fit of remorse. No doubt he'll claim the bones came from a squirrel or something. But they're a start, and they prove Mr Armstrong was right about this bone bed.

Saturday August 20th

We found a femur today. It's similar in size to a human thigh bone but shaped like some of the ones in Mr Armstrong's journals. Tonight I've been thumbing through them and trying to find an exact match. If I can't, I'll be able to say I've discovered a new dinosaur on my first try.

Tuesday August 23rd

I now have four ribs, three neck vertebrae, five sharp teeth, three claws and the front and back limbs of an animal.

In one of Mr Armstrong's journals, there's an account of a brilliant French scientist who can tell what an entire creature was like from just a single bone.

I have a few bones to work from, so I should have a pretty good idea. It's smaller than some of the other dinosaurs. If I could put a lead on it and walk it around, it would probably come up to my waist. It would also get me into trouble, because it would eat every cat and dog in sight.

It has long back limbs and short front ones, so I think it moved around on the back ones and grabbed things with the front ones. The sharp teeth and claws make me think it was after living creatures rather than plants, which is why I'd fear for the pets.

I'm building up a good picture of my dinosaur now. I'm even growing quite attached to it, though I know it would leap up and rip my throat out if I tried to cuddle it.

Wednesday August 24th

I've compared my dinosaur to all the diagrams in Mr Armstrong's journals, and I'm pretty sure it's a new one. It would be easier to tell for sure if I could find the creature's skull, but we've run out of time here. Tomorrow, we make for the third stop, Hell Creek. I really hope the next bone bed has more fossils, but even if it doesn't, we've made a good find. It might not be the biggest dinosaur ever, and it might not be complete, but at least it will be easy to fit in our trunk and take back home. If I have nothing else to show the men from the Geological Society, I'll still count this trip a success.

GET REAL

The small dinosaur Ann has found is now known as Coelophysis. She's right about it being a carnivore, as it ate small reptiles. It was discovered in 1881 by David Baldwin, a fossil hunter who worked for both Othniel Charles Marsh and Edward Drinker Cope, the two great rivals behind the late nineteenth century 'Bone Wars'.

*Thursday August 25*ᵗʰ

It seems my curse has followed me across the ocean after all.

As we were waiting for the train, I checked inside our trunk.

Every single one of the dinosaur bones had smashed into small fragments.

Father tried to comfort me by saying the bones must have been very fragile after all that time in the ground. I knew this was wrong. I've spent the last few days handling them, and while they were quite light and hollow, they weren't in any danger of disintegrating.

When Father saw it wasn't convincing me, he tried to blame it on himself by pretending he'd been careless when carrying the trunk.

I watched him carry it and he wasn't. And at any rate, I don't think the bones fell apart. I think someone smashed them.

We left the trunk with the rest of our cases in the boarding house store room last night. Our room was two floors up, so we wouldn't have heard if anyone had opened the trunk and broken the bones.

But why would they do it?

Perhaps they were a local who hates visitors coming to the town, or a drunken vandal. But why target our bones? They're only valuable to us.

I don't suppose it really matters. The important thing is that my bad luck has returned. I shall just have to hope it stays away from now on.

Friday August 26ᵗʰ

Hell's Creek is living up to its name in terms of temperature, but the bone bed more than

makes up for it. We had to walk for two miles
across flat, scorching land to get to the place Mr
Armstrong had marked, but it was worth it.

We came across the end of a thigh bone in this
morning's dig, but it was so huge we didn't
manage to get it out of the ground until late
this evening.

It reached above Father's waist when he stood
next to it, and he's not a short man. It needed
both of us to carry it back, and the woman
who runs the boarding house
gave us a funny look when we
asked if we could store it in
the hallway. If we find a full

skeleton of this beast, I have no idea how we'll get it back home. But I'll make a raft out of it and paddle home if I have to. Anything to wave this massive bone in the faces of Sir Leopold Pinkerton Hamilton and his friends.

Monday August 29ᵗʰ

This morning we unearthed what I thought was a shin bone, but I soon discovered that it tapered towards the end.

We finished removing it this evening, and it turned out to be some kind of horn. It's almost as big as the thigh, so it can't have come from any living animal.

This is exciting. There's nothing like this in any of Mr Armstrong's journals. If this is a new dinosaur, it must be one of the most remarkable ones of all.

Tuesday August 30ᵗʰ

I've pieced much of the creature's skull together now, and I was right about it being very distinctive. I think the complete skull would be about six feet long. If this is from the same creature as the thigh bone, its proportions must have been bizarre. Maybe its head was very big compared to its body, or maybe it had lots of legs, like a caterpillar.

As far as I can tell, the creature had two large horns on either side of its head. There was another horn on the end of its nose, which was shorter and wider. Its skull flattened out into a plate with pointy bits on the end.

It's a shame the skull is broken, but it at least means we'll be able to get it home. We'll carry the trunk out tomorrow morning and bring the skull pieces back in the evening. Then we can move on to our next stop, Black Canyon.

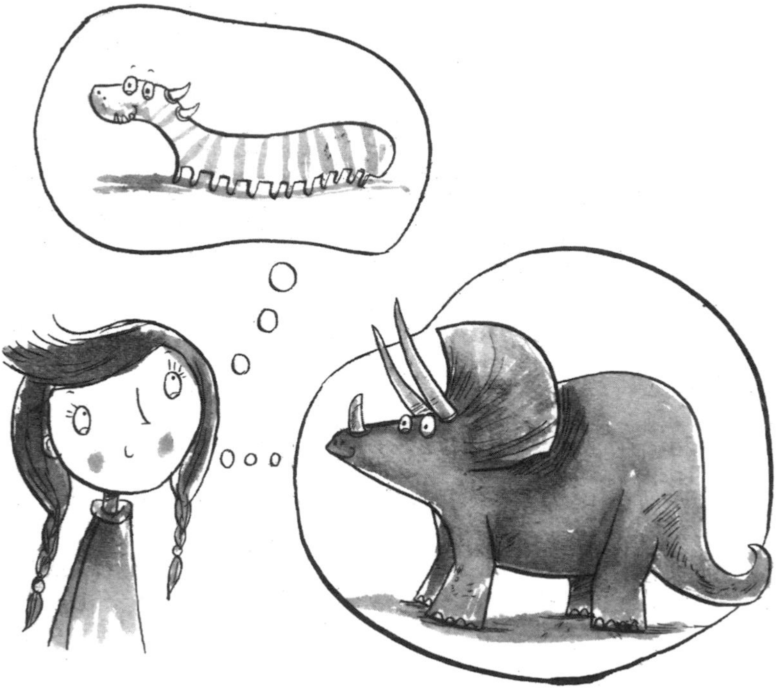

GET REAL

The skull Ann has found belongs to the creature now known as Triceratops. It was a large plant-eating dinosaur that lived around 68 million years ago. It's one of the most recognisable dinosaurs, thanks to its three horns and the bony frill around the back of its head.

The neck frill might have helped it to defend itself against its main predator, Tyrannosaurus rex, or it might have regulated body temperature. Another theory is that the frills were used for displays of dominance, like the antlers in animals such as reindeer.

Triceratops was identified by Othniel Charles Marsh after specimens were sent to him by bone collectors. At first he thought the horns must have belonged to an extinct buffalo, but he soon realised they were from a dinosaur.

Chapter 5

A Dangerous Expedition

Wednesday August 31st

Today my dreadful curse struck again. I spent the morning searching for the rest of the creature's remains, but found nothing. I still had my thigh bone and the impressive skull, so I had no reason to be frustrated.

We managed to fit all the skull pieces into the trunk, except for the thigh bone and tusk, which we tied to the top.

We were on our way back to our boarding house when we heard hooves thundering behind us. Three men were approaching on horseback.

Before long they were circling us and kicking up a huge cloud of dust.

When they came to a halt, I asked them what they wanted. One of them took a pistol out of his holster and pointed it at us while the others untied cloth sacks and held them out.

'Give us what's inside your trunk,' said the first man. 'Do it fast.'

Despite the peril of our situation, I couldn't stop myself laughing. The bandits must have thought they'd struck gold by chancing across a pair of tourists carrying their luggage through the desert. I couldn't wait to see their faces when they found out what we were actually carrying.

We placed the trunk on the floor and Father opened it up. I smiled at the man with the gun and shrugged.

Instead of rolling his eyes and admitting his mistake, the first bandit simply said, 'In the sacks.'

'These are just old bones,' I said. I tried to sound calm, but I could hear my voice wavering. 'There are hundreds more in the ground around here.'

The man just pointed his gun to the empty sack, and then back at us.

'Please let us go,' said Father. 'These old scraps aren't worth anything.'

It was true. The broken skull of an ancient creature would be worth nothing to these bandits. It wouldn't even make an interesting curiosity to wager in a card game. Yet to me, it meant everything. It was a piece of solid evidence of an entirely new creature that I could take back to the Geological Society.

The bandit just stared at us in silence. I expected his expression wouldn't change if he pulled

the trigger. It was probably something he'd done a hundred times before.

I loved the broken skull, but it wasn't worth being killed for. I carried the pieces over from the trunk into the cloth sacks. At every stage, I was expecting the men to realise they were stealing something worthless and give up. But it never happened. Eventually, I'd handed all the pieces over. The bandits tied the sacks to their horses and galloped away.

We trudged back to our boarding house as the men rode out of sight and my precious skull disappeared with them.

Thursday September I[st]

We have carried on to our next stop, Black Canyon. What else could we do?

I am now convinced my bad luck will strike at every turn. Every time I make a discovery, cruel fate will snatch it away. But I cannot simply admit defeat and go home. I shall have to carry on, even if further disaster awaits.

All I've ever wanted is to be a great fossil collector. If I waste six months and all our savings only to return home empty-handed, I shall officially be the worst in the world.

But I must keep trying to escape my terrible curse.

Sunday September 4th

We have enjoyed a spell of cooler weather, which has allowed us to work through the day. No success so far, however. The spot Mr Armstrong marked as a bone bed has yielded only dull rocks. I must force myself to keep

going, and try not to think about the wonderful skull the bandits stole.

Tuesday September 6th

Just two days before we are due to leave, we have finally found something. This morning I struck upon a large, flat bone I hoped would be part of another three-horned skull. But it turned out to be the pelvis of an altogether different creature. Soon afterwards I found a toe bone, a thigh bone, four teeth and several fragments of rib. This is a very large dinosaur, one that would tower far above humans if it were still alive.

After consulting Mr Armstrong's journals, I can conclude that we've found yet another new species. That's three major discoveries in just four locations. This truly is a country rich in brilliant fossils. If only my bad luck hadn't pursued me here.

GET REAL

The dinosaur Ann has discovered is Allosaurus, a predator that lived in the late Jurassic period. It had strong hind limbs, a long tail and teeth that curved backwards so it could hold onto prey. Scientists have recently found evidence that Allosaurus battled Stegosaurus, which would be a good fight to pull up a seat and watch if you ever invent a time machine.

Wednesday September 7th

Once again, we have been hit by the curse. And once again we must move on to our next destination without our precious bones.

I kept on working until late last night. I managed to find a few more of the sharp, curved teeth and an intact rib. I felt as though a skull must be close, but I gave up as the sun began to set.

The trunk was very heavy with all the bones inside, so we made slow progress back to our boarding house. There was an astonishing orange sunset ahead of us, but I would have traded it for a glimpse of ancient skull.

When I heard horses approaching, I thought we may be under attack by bandits again. But when I glanced over my shoulder I saw it was just a wooden wagon covered in dirty white cloth. I didn't think they could want anything with us, so I kept on walking.

The wagon pulled up alongside us and the rider shouted, 'Hey!' He peered at us with his small black eyes. His face was matted with dust and he was missing a lot of his teeth. A woman who was sitting next to him had her face set into a tight squint as though she was staring into the sun. Flies were swarming around her dark shirt, and she made no effort to brush them away.

'That them?' she asked.

'Must be,' said the man.

Father waved at them. 'I'm not sure who you think we are, but there's been a huge misunderstanding,' he said. 'We are visitors from England and we mean you no harm.'

The man turned to his side and spat before fixing his eyes back on Father.

Father took his hat off and bowed. 'It's been lovely to meet you, but if you don't mind we'll be on our way.'

The man pointed at the trunk and said, 'Open it.'

I pushed the lid open and the couple peered inside.

'That's them alright,' said the woman.

Someone else was shuffling around in the dark space of the wagon. There was a metallic clack and an old lady with wild grey hair sprung forward. She was pointing a huge rifle right at Father.

'Grave robbin' scum!' she shouted.

'You've got it wrong,' said Father. 'We're nothing of the sort.' He held his hands above his head and I noticed they were quaking.

'We know what you been doing,' said the man. 'We found the earth on our family grave disturbed. We spoke to a gentleman who was passing, and he said he'd seen two folks just like you stealing the bones. He said we'd catch you if we was fast.'

The woman let out a loud sob and the man squeezed her hand. The old lady scowled at us and clasped the rifle's trigger. Even the horse seemed to be frowning.

'Anyway, we've caught you now,' said the man. 'We don't know what you're doing with the bones but...'

'I know what they're doing,' said the old woman. 'Witchcraft!'

'I'm not a witch!' I said.

'That's exactly what a witch would say!' yelled the old woman. There were only a couple of teeth left in her dark gums.

I pointed into the trunk. 'These bones are far too big to be from your family plot. Look...'

I reached into the case and the woman let out another sob. I held one of the thigh bones next to me, and it came all the way up to my chest.

'See?' I asked. 'It's from a lizard, not a human.'

The man stared at it in confusion. The woman stopped sobbing and wiped her red eyes.

'She's put a spell on them,' said the old lady. 'Probably trying to bring them back to life but made them grow instead.'

The man put his hand on the end of her rifle and forced it down. 'No,' he said. 'I reckon she's telling the truth. Even Uncle Abraham wasn't that tall.'

'Why would there be lizards round here anyway?' asked the old lady. 'Unless a witch summoned them.'

'Maybe so,' said the man. 'But it's none of our business. We've got enough problems of our own without witches and lizards.' He fixed his tiny eyes on me. 'You can go.'

I breathed a sigh of relief and grabbed my side of the trunk.

'Leave the bones here,' said the old lady. 'I want to check in case there are some you ain't bewitched yet.'

I was about to argue back when I saw Father scooping the bones out.

'Let's cut our losses,' he said. 'We've got out

of this without taking any rifle blasts. I'd say
that was a good result.'

I supposed he was right.

When Father had finished removing our
precious finds, we picked up the empty case and
trudged back.

As we were going, I turned back to the family.

'What did the man look like?' I asked. 'The
one who said we'd been robbing your graves?'

'About as tall as me,' said the man. 'Maybe a
little older. He had a white moustache.'

*Thursday September 8*th
There was no sign of a man with a white

moustache in the town. I thought he might have been an angry old local, determined to turn everyone against us tourists, but there was no one fitting the description. All the men I saw were too young for white hair and the only people they were angry with were their fellow card players.

Maybe it doesn't matter who set the family against us. Our efforts will result in disaster whatever we do, because of my curse.

Oh well. At least our next destination, Midway, should be free of unfortunate incidents. According to Mr Armstrong's notes, there's nothing but a few small boarding houses, a saloon, a store and some private houses. It was all set up for men working on the railway, and now the work is complete it may become a ghost town. Surely it's the sort of place where I can

dig for bones without getting hassled by violent bandits or mad locals.

GET REAL

There are many abandoned towns or 'ghost towns' in the American West. Some grew rapidly and were abandoned in just a few months. This was often because the town was built around a resource that ran out. An example is Bodie in California, which sprung up around a silver mine. The town had 2,000 buildings and 10,000 inhabitants at its height, but swiftly became a ghost town when the silver was gone.

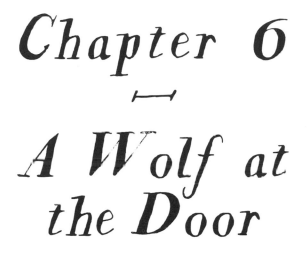

Chapter 6

A Wolf at the Door

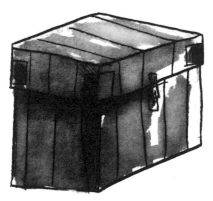

Friday September 9th

Midway is just as quiet as we were expecting.
The bone bed Mr Armstrong marked is only a
few hundred yards from the boarding house,
which itself is just a few hundred yards from
the rail station.

We've found nothing yet. But if we do, at least
I can be confident of getting it onto the train
without running into thieves.

Father is already snoring away behind me,
leaving me with nothing to do but look back
over this journal.

I see that a man with a white moustache spoke
to Father on the train platform in New York.
Could this be the same man who told the family
we'd been stealing from their graves?

I doubt it. He wouldn't have followed us all the

way from New York just to play a practical joke. And Father seemed to think he was very nice.

But what if someone has been behind all the things that have happened to us? Reading back over my diary, I wonder if my belief in my curse has blinded me. Maybe it hasn't all been bad luck. Maybe it's been sabotage.

Sunday September 11ᵗʰ

The Midway bone bed has now yielded its treasure. We moved our dig location a few yards to the right and soon a huge knot of bone emerged. I knew it was some sort of vertebra, but I couldn't imagine where it would fit into a full skeleton. It was only when I discovered more just like it that I realised I was looking at the parts of a long, flexible neck.

Monday September 12ᵗʰ

Today we discovered some tail vertebrae from the same creature. The beast must have been over a hundred feet long. No sign of the legs yet, but whatever they looked like, it must have been very strange. It seems impossible that such a thing could have walked the Earth. Yet the evidence is all right here. These finds could change the way everyone thinks about life on Earth – if I ever manage to get any of them home.

GET REAL

The massive creature Ann has discovered is the Diplodocus. They were a type of plant-eating dinosaur known as sauropods, that had long necks and tails, small heads and thick legs. Illustrations usually show them reaching up with their long necks to eat leaves, but in truth scientists can't agree on how flexible their necks were. Some think they could move them around freely, while others believe they were held in a fixed position and they had to rear up on their hind legs to reach tall trees.

Tuesday September 13th

I've found a skull which I think fits with the neck and tail bones, but it's not very big. If this is indeed the right one, the creature must have looked very funny lumbering around with its tiny head.

I asked Father to lay the creature's bones out on the ground this evening while I continued my dig. When he'd done it, I noticed he'd put the skull on the tail instead of the neck. I'll have to be sure he doesn't do that in front of the Geological Society. A mistake like that could ruin my reputation forever.

GET REAL

Placing a skull at the end of a creature's tail might seem like a basic error, but it was made by one of the most famous fossil hunters of all. When Edward Drinker Cope was reconstructing a sea reptile named the 'Elasmosaurus' in 1868, he thought its head would have been at the end of its short tail rather than its long neck. He assumed the long tail would have been used to propel it through the water.

Wednesday September 14th

The more I think about it, the more convinced I become that someone has been meddling with us. And tonight, I'm going to find out who.

This evening we carried our new fossils back to our boarding house in the trunk and examined them on the ground outside. If anyone is spying on us, they'll have seen our new finds.

I'm going to make it easy for them. I've left the trunk just inside the unlocked entrance to the boarding house. Instead of going to sleep, I'll watch it from a chair in the hallway.

At worst, I'll miss out on a night of sleep. But if it works, I'll finally catch our tormentor.

Thursday September 15th

We have now abandoned our schedule. We are heading back east on the railroad, towards New York, with an empty trunk. Father is still shaken from what happened last night, and we need to discuss what we're going to do next.

There are two hours before our train stops at Black Canyon. I need to talk to Father soon, but first I want to get down everything that happened last night.

Rather than going upstairs, I pulled a wooden chair into the gloom at the end of the hallway and watched the trunk.

I sat and stared at it for hour after hour. Every time I felt myself nodding off I shifted in the chair so I was less comfortable. I wanted to be wide awake when our enemy emerged.

I listened for footsteps but could hear nothing except the distant cries of coyotes outside and Father's snores from the floor above.

A voice in my head told me I was wasting my time. That everything that had gone wrong was simply down to my curse and that it would be better to get some sleep. I ignored it and kept staring at the trunk.

Eventually I couldn't help it. My head lolled forward and I fell asleep. I dreamt the dinosaurs had come back to life and I was chasing them across the desert. Every time I got close to one I would stumble to the dusty ground. After one such imaginary fall I jolted awake to see the handle of the front door turning.

My heart was still racing from the dream and I thought I might be imagining things. But the door opened and a tall figure crept in. He passed the hall window and I saw his thin white moustache.

The man stopped in front of my trunk and unfurled a large cloth sack. Then he slowly opened the lid. He smiled and lifted one of the tail bones out.

I stood up and stepped forward.

'What do you want with my bones?' I asked.

The man with the white moustache jumped, dropping the bone.

'Please excuse me,' he said, backing towards the door. 'I mistook them for the remains of my Uncle Charles.'

'You used a lie like that before,' I said.

'When you told that family from Black Canyon that we were robbing their graves.'

'I'm afraid I have no idea what you're talking about, young lady,' said the man. 'Perhaps you've mistaken me for someone else.'

He looked genuinely confused and in my sleepy state I wondered if this really was a misunderstanding. I had to remind myself that I'd caught him in the act of stealing.

'Did you pay the bandits in Hell's Creek to come after us too?' I asked.

'I don't follow,' said the man. 'You seem to be up very late, so why don't you run along to bed?'

There were heavy steps behind me. Father was coming down the stairs.

He squinted at the man. 'You?' he asked. 'Chap from the station in New York? What on earth are you doing out here?'

'Okay,' said the man. 'I'll admit it. We have met before. And thanks for blabbing the truth in that station. I had a pretty good idea who you were, but your careless talk confirmed my suspicions.'

'He's been following us all along,' I said. 'He's the one who's been sabotaging our whole expedition.'

'I'll soon teach him about that,' said Father, rolling his sleeves up and holding his fists out.

The man lifted aside his coat, pulled out a handgun and pointed it at us. Father's hands drooped back down.

'Of course I've been tailing you,' said the man. 'Do you think I would let a little schoolgirl like you steal my glory?'

'What glory?' I asked. 'Who are you?'

'The greatest fossil man in the world,' he
said. 'I've watched your digs with great interest.
Your first find was fairly unremarkable,
hardly the sort of thing that would help my
reputation. I didn't think the bones were worth
sending back East, so I simply hammered them
to pieces. Your other finds have been truly
magnificent, however. Soon all the world will
know about them, and they'll know them as my
discoveries.'

'But how did you know about our trip?' I
asked.

'Oh come on,' said the man. 'I know
you're uneducated, but at least try and show
some intelligence.'

He took a letter out of his pocket. I recognised

it straight away. It was one of the pleas for
financial help to the American universities.

'I'm Professor Edwin Wolf of Harvard
University,' said the man. 'You wrote to me,
remember? At first I dismissed your ideas as
the fancies of a young girl with an overactive
imagination, but the more I studied the maps, the
more I thought you were right about bone beds
in the West. I decided to follow you from New
York and watch from a distance. If you discovered
nothing, I'd have wasted a few weeks. But if you
discovered something important, I could take it as
easily as candy from a baby.'

He shoved the letter back into his pocket.

'If you thought we were right about the bone
beds, why didn't you offer to join us?' I asked. 'We
could have dug together, and presented our finds
to the world together.'

His cheeks flushed red and the gun trembled in his hand. I was worried he might squeeze the trigger without meaning to.

'Can you imagine what my colleagues would say if they found I'd needed the assistance of a little girl?' he asked. 'That wouldn't make my reputation. It would destroy it.'

He took a series of deep breaths and the gun fell still again.

'But there's no need to worry about it now,' he said. 'I've already sent your other finds back east. I shall present them to the American Geological Society later this year, and they shall be named the 'great wolfosaurus' and the 'three-horned wolfosaurus'. You should forget the rest of your schedule as I shall examine the two final bone beds on your list to see if there

are any other fossils that could further my impending fame. In fact, I strongly advise you to return to New York right away and await your crossing home. If I see you again I'll shoot you without hesitation.'

He lifted the rest of our bones into his sack, smiled and went out.

'This country is truly full of scoundrels,' said Father. 'We should never have come.'

'We'll know we discovered those dinosaurs,' I said. 'Even if no one else does.'

We went to our room and packed, then we waited at the station for this train. I think that's everything. Now to talk to Father.

Friday September 16th

We now risk our lives with every step we take. That's because we didn't head back to New York as Professor Wolf commanded. Instead, we changed trains at Black Canyon and went West again. We passed back through Midway, and then through Rock Spring, which was meant to be our next stop. We carried on to the final bone bed, Pine Bluff.

At first I wanted to carry on with our schedule as planned, but Father refused. He said he wanted to return to New York, as we'd only had a brief stay last time and he felt like seeing more of it. Hmm. I don't remember him being so keen on the place before Professor Wolf threatened us.

When I announced I'd rather be shot than leave this country without an amazing fossil,

we came to a compromise. We would travel straight on to the final bone bed at Pine Bluff, get all we could from it, and leave on Wednesday, one day before Professor Wolf was due to arrive.

Saturday September 17th

Our gamble has been worth it so far. The bone bed here in Pine Bluff is the best of all. I struck a large thigh bone soon after we began last night, which I think comes from the same type of creature we discovered in Black Canyon. This morning I began to uncover the skull pieces of another of those three-horned dinosaurs. That means two of my three major finds are back. Even if Professor Wolf claims these discoveries as his own while we sail home, we'll still have the first examples outside America.

Father paced back and forth all day, keeping watch for Professor Wolf. I'm sure the bone bed at Rock Spring will keep that villain occupied until we leave here on Wednesday. But even if it doesn't, I'm enjoying this dig far too much to quit.

If this is my last diary entry, it means Professor Wolf has caught up with us and made good on his threat.

Sunday September 18th

The problem with this bone bed is that it's just too good. Today I discovered neck vertebrae like the ones from the Midway site, as well as fragments of shin bones and ribs that I think are from the same creature. My new finds have made up for all the discoveries that Professor Wolf stole from me, but they've created a new problem. How are we going to get them all home? I've already got too much to fit in the trunk.

Rather disappointingly, Father stayed back at our boarding house today. He said it was because he was tired, but I know it's really because he's scared of Professor Wolf. I don't blame him, I just wish he would be more honest about it.

I feel a little worried too. Every now and then I'll spot something out of the corner of my eye and think it's Professor Wolf stalking towards me with his gun raised. But as soon as I get back to the fabulous bone bed I forget all about the danger.

Monday September 19th
Today I uncovered a new creature that wasn't at any of the other sites. It's also unlike

anything I've seen in Mr Armstrong's journals.
In fact, it's unlike anything I've seen anywhere.

The first things I discovered were large bony
plates that tapered to a point at the end.
I wondered if I'd found some sort of ancient
turtle. But then I uncovered a brilliantly
preserved row of ribs next to them and saw it
was another dinosaur.

From the way the plates and ribs were
arranged, it looks as though the creature had a
row of hard spikes on its back. But what would
be the point of that? If the plates were for
armour, what good would they do there?

I have no idea, but I'm glad I got to it before
Professor Wolf could. This fearsome beast
deserves better than to become known as the
'spiky-backed wolfosaurus'.

I really hope there isn't another one in the ground around here for Professor Wolf to dig up when he arrives. Even though all my other discoveries have been stolen, I'll still have this one. Just one find as good as this will be enough for my name to go down in fossil-hunting history.

I took the spiky monster's bones back to our room and piled them on top of the others. I have far too many to take back, but I can't bear to leave any behind.

If I have to choose one lot of remains, I suppose it will have to be the one from today. But it would break my heart to leave the three-horned dinosaur behind. That's my favourite of all. I told Father about my problem tonight, but he didn't say anything. He's so worried about Professor Wolf catching up with us, he just wants me to decide so we can go.

GET REAL

Ann has found the remains of a
Stegosaurus, a large plant-eating dinosaur
with two rows of bony plates along its
back.

Scientists don't agree exactly what the
plates were for. It's possible they helped
to defend against predators, though they
would only have protected a limited area.
They might also have deterred enemies
by making the creature seem even bigger
than it was. Some researchers have also
suggested that the plates helped to regulate
body temperature.

As well as its back plates, Stegosaurus is
famed for having a very small brain in
relation to its overall size. Despite its vast
bulk, it had the same size of brain as a
dog. But unlike a dog, it wouldn't have
been much use at fetching sticks or rolling
over to let you rub its belly.

Chapter 7

Return to England

Tuesday September 20th

I take back everything I said about Father. He
wasn't cowering in our boarding house after
all. For the past two days he's actually been
in the town's saloon bar winning money from
local miners at Three Card Monte. I asked him
if he'd been using the dealing trick he taught
himself, but he denied it. I don't believe him,
and it's just as well we have to leave town
tomorrow. Professor Wolf won't be the only
one trying to shoot us if the locals find out he's
cheated them.

Father let some of the players give him their
luggage instead of money. As a result, we now
have enough trunk space to take almost all my
finds home, and we can also afford to pay the
train guards to stow them all.

I couldn't quite fit all the bones into our new
trunks, though. I still have a skull, a tail, some

ribs, six legs and a few of those bony plates. I've thought of something I can do with them, but I don't have much time, so I'll have to leave this entry for now.

Wednesday September 21ˢᵗ

We had to take the short trip from our boarding house to the train stop four times this morning because of all our new luggage. Our journey home will no doubt contain much more inconvenience. But it will all be worth it when I show the Geological Society my fossils.

We waited on the far end of the platform as the train pulled in, so that the guard could show us where to store our things.

The train chugged in, came to a stop, and the passengers stepped out. I was gazing at

them when I spotted something that made my heart stop.

A white moustache.

Professor Wolf was there. He'd arrived a day earlier than we expected, on the very train we planned to leave on.

I looked around for Father, but he was nowhere to be seen. I didn't blame him for running away, but had no idea how he could have vanished so quickly.

The lid of one of the trunks at my feet creaked open and I saw Father's pale, terrified face inside. He pointed to the next case along and snapped the lid shut.

Without thinking, I leapt in. I immediately

regretted the one I'd picked, as it was full of tail vertebrae from the long dinosaur. At least I hadn't bedded down in the trunk of spiky back plates.

I lay on the knots of bone, listening to the footsteps going past and praying that Professor Wolf wouldn't fling the lid open and draw his gun.

Two people approached and my case was swept up. The rail porters muttered about how heavy it was as they placed it in the carriage. I wondered how they'd react when they tried to lift Father's case. He must be twice as heavy as me.

In the end, it took them four tries to lug it up. They were soon panting and muttering about how they don't get paid enough to handle luggage that could break their backs.

The rest of our trunks were piled in soon afterwards, and the train pulled away. I let out a deep sigh. We'd managed to escape Professor Wolf, and now it was time to find our seats and begin the long journey home.

I tried to push the lid of the case. Nothing happened. I tried again.

I could hear Father's voice above the chugging train. 'I think they've put the other trunks on top on ours!' he shouted. 'How long is it until our stop?'

'A few hours,' I said. 'I forget how long exactly.' I hadn't forgotten. It was six hours. I had six whole hours to try and make myself comfortable on some knotty tail bones.

The trunk grew hotter as the day wore on, and soon I was wiping sweat from my brow. I fought the urge to bang my fists against the lid and scream. I had the horrible feeling that my bad luck had struck again and I would starve or die of exhaustion inside the sweltering case.

I told myself to snap out of it. If it hadn't been

for my silly belief in the curse, I'd have realised someone was disrupting our trip much sooner. I wasn't cursed. I was lucky.

Lucky to have found some amazing bones and lucky to be heading home to share them with experts. All I had to do was survive one horrible journey.

I was about to ask Father how he was coping when I heard snoring from his trunk. Not too badly, then.

By the time we finally arrived in Rock Spring I was so weak I couldn't even cry for help as I waited for the station porters to reach us.

'What's in these?' I heard one of them ask as they lugged the box on top of mine away.

'Bones,' said another man.

'Nobody said anything about dead bodies,'
said the first man. 'They ought to pay us extra.'

I tried to push the lid of my trunk open, but I
was still too feeble. I only managed to squeeze
my fingers out from underneath the lid.
The first man gasped. 'They're coming back
to life,' he whispered. 'Must be some sort of
voodoo magic.'

'Don't be dumb,' said the second man.
He stepped over and threw open the top of
my trunk.

I managed to sit up, but when I tried to speak
all that came out was a low moan. The men
looked at each other, screamed and ran away.
I suppose I must have looked like a reanimated
corpse with my pale skin and tired eyes, so I
can understand the confusion. But grown men

should know that dead bodies don't really come back to life, so I have little sympathy.

I'm pleased to say that after much water and rest, Father and I are now fully recovered. I'm considering reporting the cowardly porters to their superiors, but it would be too difficult to

explain why we were travelling inside trunks of bones in the first place.

Tomorrow we shall store our luggage, take our seats and continue our return journey in greater comfort.

Tuesday November 1ˢᵗ

We arrived back in Bristol this morning. I must admit to a certain relief on returning to the gloomy English climate after the heat of the New World. The slate grey skies and light drizzle were a real comfort as we made our way to the railway station.

Rather than getting off at Bath and taking a carriage home, we decided to carry straight on to London and show our finds to Mr Armstrong. I'm sure he'll be just as excited about the bones as I am, and I can't wait to share them.

Wednesday November 2nd

It took us so long to find a carriage that would take all our trunks that we didn't reach Mr Armstrong's house until after midnight.

We had to wake up Mrs Baker, and her mood turned even fouler when she saw all of our trunks.

'The last thing we need is more of them lizard bones,' she said as we carried the cases up the narrow stairway. 'If you ask me, it'll serve him right if lizards steal his bones after he dies.'

Mr Armstrong was overjoyed when he saw our finds, and he clapped his hands together over and over again as I showed them to him. He stayed up for the whole night to examine them, but you would never have known to see him at breakfast. His passion for the fossils had

energised him more than the strongest coffee
ever could.

He confirmed that we'd discovered some
new species, and he proposed the names
Triceratops, Diplodocus, Allosaurus and
Stegosaurus. I warned him that all but the
latter would probably be named after Professor
Wolf, but he thinks we may still have a chance
to claim the beasts if we act fast.

He's arranged a meeting of the Geological
Society on Saturday, and he's sure that even
the stuffiest old members won't dismiss me
this time.

That gives me just a few days to prepare my
new speech. I won't attempt a long introduction
this time, I'll just go straight to my finds and let
my dinosaurs do the talking.

Thursday November 3rd

I returned Mr Armstrong's map and journals
today, and I read him some entries from
this diary.

He apologised over and over again for putting
me in contact with Professor Wolf. He says
the world of bone hunting is cursed with more
barbarity than the dinosaurs themselves were
capable of. He's going to write to his friend
Professor Godwin at Yale University and tell
him all about what happened. He'll soon spread
the word about Professor Wolf among the fossil
experts of the New World, which should tarnish
his reputation and maybe even discredit
his finds.

I hope he succeeds. I already feel sorry for those
poor creatures for being extinct. The last thing
they need is to be named after Professor Wolf.

Saturday November 5ᵗʰ

This afternoon we took the trunks down to the
Geological Society and I pieced each species
together as best as I could. Then I covered them
up with blankets so I could reveal them one
by one.

I decided to start with the Stegosaurus fossil
as it's the one Professor Wolf might not have.
Even if the scientists lost interest after five
minutes, it would be recorded that I discovered
Stegosaurus. After that strong start, I'd show
them the Allosaurus, then the Diplodocus,
before building up to my showstopper, the
Triceratops.

As I watched Mr Armstrong open the doors and
usher the scientists in, I noticed the same three
old men taking their seats on the front row. Sir
Leopold Pinkerton Hamilton sat in the middle,

with Sir Fitzhugh Xavier Sapping to his left and Sir Hobart Remmington Risewell to his right. Their pained faces gave me a brief stab of doubt. Perhaps even my amazing finds wouldn't be enough to win them over.

'This is what you call an emergency meeting for?' shouted Sir Leopold Pinkerton Hamilton. 'More infantile fantasies?'

'I think you'll be very interested in what she has to show,' said Mr Armstrong, clapping his hands together. 'And I'm sure a respected scientist such as yourself will wait to see the evidence before passing judgement.'

Sir Leopold stared at me with a look of distaste, as though he had unexpectedly eaten something sour.

When everyone had taken their seats, I

announced that I had just returned from the American West.

'Ghastly place,' muttered Sir Fitzhugh Xavier Sapping. 'I hear that every creature over there is as small and wretched as a dormouse. Even their lions are weaker than our kittens.'

I decided to get straight on with revealing the bones before any more ill-informed chatter could break out. I whipped the blanket away from the Stegosaurus bones and went through them. There was a murmur of excitement when I showed them the back plates.

'Stuff and nonsense,' shouted Sir Hobart Remmington Risewell. 'Those are clearly the remains of a turtle that died fighting a lizard. Tenacious chaps, turtles.'

'Or maybe a dog with spikes on its back,'

muttered Sir Leopold Pinkerton Hamilton. 'I saw one just like that while my glasses were being mended.'

This time the others took no notice. They weren't really paying much attention to what I was saying either, to be honest. They were transfixed by the bones. Many had risen from their seats, and were jostling to get a better look.

When I pulled the cloth away from the Allosaurus, some of the scientists at the back stood on their seats. One even overbalanced with excitement and had to be helped outside to take some air.

When I whipped away the blanket covering the Diplodocus, they could contain themselves no more. They rushed to the front, desperate to get closer to the amazing beasts.

Sir Leopold Pinkerton Hamilton, Sir Hobart
Remmington Risewell and Sir Fitzhugh Xavier
Sapping remained seated with their arms
folded, muttering angrily about dogs and
turtles. But all the others crowded around me,
yelling questions from all directions.

Mr Armstrong had to raise his voice like a strict
schoolmaster to make them sit down so I could
finish. When I was finally done, I was given
a hearty round of applause. It made quite a
change from my last presentation, which was
greeted only by the sound of people leaving.

We stayed in the hall until late this evening.
None of the men would leave until they'd had
a chance to discuss the finds with me, and at
least five of them promised to submit papers to
scientific journals naming me as the finder of
the beasts.

By the end of the night, even Sir Leopold Pinkerton Hamilton was starting to admit that my discoveries were significant, though he had the nerve to claim that a trained researcher would have been able to uncover even better ones if they'd been in the west of America.

Mr Armstrong told me not to worry about it, as Sir Leopold never admits he was wrong about anything. Soon he'll be claiming he was the only one in the room who understood the importance of the fossils.

Sir Leopold Pinkerton Hamilton and the others have promised to give Mr Armstrong some money to open a museum dedicated to ancient fossils, and he wants my creatures to have a starring role. Mr Armstrong even thinks ordinary members of the general public should be allowed in, though not everyone agrees with him.

I was happy to leave my monsters with Mr
Armstrong, even though I have grown a little
attached to them. It would be wonderful if he
could put them on display for the ordinary
men and women of London. The more we
nurture a love for fossils, the more people
will get involved and the more creatures we'll
discover. Despite what some members of the
Society would say, you need nothing more than
a hammer to begin a career as a bone hunter.
I'm proof of that.

I'm glad we're returning home tomorrow, even
if the Stegosaurus and his friends are staying
here. I enjoyed my adventure in the New World,
but right now I just want to return to my cold,
rainy beach.

GET REAL

London's Natural History Museum opened in 1881. Richard Owen was in charge of the British Museum's natural history section, and felt it deserved a building of its own. Owen made the museum open to the general public rather than just the scientific elite, which was unusual at the time.

Monday December 5ᵗʰ

Two letters were delivered to Father while I was at the seafront this morning. It seems my fame is spreading:

Dear Miss Mansfield

I read of your recent finds in the New World with great interest. I wish to congratulate you wholeheartedly on your discovery of these noble British creatures. Yes – British, I say! For it is my belief that these vigorous beasts cannot be of American origin. Rather, they were animals from our own proud nation that were merely visiting the New World for a holiday and got trapped by rough weather. This would explain why they were buried in such shallow ground. Had you delved deeper, I have no doubt you would have chanced upon some more pathetic American fossils.

Congratulations once again and God save the Queen!

Professor Welton Stanway Kibble

Dear Miss Mansfield

Hoorah for your recent finds in the New World. I assume you failed to bring back my bison, coyote and opossum. But let us not worry about that, as your excellent dinosaurs more than make up for it. But please bear me in mind if you should ever find a dinosaur egg. I'd love to see the look on old Meredith's face when he spots me scoffing a soft-boiled Stegosaurus egg for breakfast.

Yours sincerely

Professor Ignacio Baldry Fitzsimons

I'm so glad Mr Armstrong is fighting to let members of the public into his museum. If these men represent the scientific elite, my creatures deserve better.

Saturday December 17th

I was sifting through the rocks on the beach this afternoon when Father came running over. He said he had some surprising news, and I assumed he'd sold some of the bones to a tourist for a very high price.

But he led me home, and I was amazed to find Mr Armstrong waiting for us. He'd come all the way from London to see me.

Apparently, my discoveries are the talk of society, and Sir Leopold Pinkerton Hamilton is claiming the entire expedition was his idea. But Mr Armstrong doesn't mind, as he's given him full funding for the museum. He can even afford to give up his job as a surgeon to run it, and the room housing my creatures is to be named after me.

I must arrange another trip to London soon, so I

can see the Stegosaurus and his friends in the 'Mansfield Gallery'.

Then Mr Armstrong handed me a letter from his friend Professor Godwin at Yale University, which contained the best news of all. Professor Godwin was appalled to hear about Professor Wolf's behaviour, and thought it would almost certainly destroy his reputation if he'd had one left to destroy. But the truth is he'd already made himself the laughing stock of the scientific world with a presentation to the American Geographic Society in October.

Professor Wolf claimed to have discovered a creature named the 'Wolfosaurus Rex'. It had six legs, a skull on the end of its tail and triangular plates lining its arms. His speech was drowned out by howls of laughter before he could share any of the genuine discoveries.

When the audience refused to take his find seriously, he suffered a fit of rage and struck some of them with the bones. He was eventually restrained and has since been thrown out of the Society and fired from his post at the university.

This has all worked out even better than I could have hoped. On our last night in Pine Bluff, I had an idea about what to do with the bones I couldn't fit in the trunks. I took them back to the site and arranged them on the ground to create an odd, imaginary creature with a skull on its tail and plates on its arms. Then I buried them with a thin layer of soil.

I'd been hoping ever since that Professor Wolf had found the bones and fallen for my hoax. At best, I thought it would make him look foolish in front of his peers. I didn't think it would lead to him violently assaulting them.

184

Professor Wolf has been cast out by the American scientists, and all his work has been discarded. That means there'll never be such a thing as 'the great wolfosaurus', 'the three-horned wolfosaurus' or 'the long-necked wolfosaurus'. Those creatures will now be known as Allosaurus, Triceratops and Diplodocus instead. And I shall be credited with discovering them.

If my fossils are causing a stir in London, I hope it encourages others to travel to the West of America and look for more. I'm sure there are hundreds of other amazing creatures waiting just beneath the ground.

The dinosaurs were the strangest and most magnificent beasts ever to walk the Earth. Now the time has come for us to find them and give them back to the world.

The End

The Fossil Hunters

Although Ann's diary is set in the year 1870, it is inspired by events that took place throughout the nineteenth century, as fossil discoveries caught the world's imagination.

The character of Ann was inspired by Mary Anning, who was born in 1799 and lived in the seaside town of Lyme Regis in Dorset, England. Mary spent her childhood picking up shells and bones on the beach to sell to visitors.

When she was 12, she helped her brother Joseph to uncover some strange remains from the nearby rocks. They thought it looked like a large crocodile, but it turned

Mary Anning

out to be the first complete skeleton of a marine reptile named Ichthyosaur. They managed to sell the fossil for £23, a huge sum of money for a poor family.

Mary went on to great success as a fossil hunter. She was highly skilled at removing bones from the rocks without damaging them. Among her most famous finds were a marine reptile called Plesiosaur and a flying reptile called a Pterosaur.

Mary died of cancer in 1847, and interest in her story has grown since her death. Despite having little money and no formal training, she became one of the most important women in the history of science.

But Mary wasn't the only remarkable fossil hunter. Gideon Mantell was a country doctor with an interest in geology. In 1822 he discovered some unusual teeth that he believed came from a huge creature that resembled the iguana, which he named Iguanodon. Mantell became obsessed with searching for ancient creatures, and soon gathered the most impressive collection of fossils in the country. But a rival emerged who was determined to outdo him.

Richard Owen was a talented and ambitious scientist, but he was known for mistreating whoever stood in his way. He claimed many of Mantell's discoveries as his own and tried to stop Mantell's research from being published.

When Mantell died, Owen even wrote an obituary that played down his achievements. But for all his faults, he made a massive contribution to the field. He coined the term 'dinosaur', and he helped found London's Natural History Museum, which meant ancient fossils could be seen by ordinary members of the public as well as by experts.

The rivalry between Owen and Mantell might have been fierce, but it was nothing compared to one that developed across the Atlantic. The 'Bone Wars' is the name given to the rush to discover and name dinosaurs in the USA in the late nineteenth century. It was driven by the conflict between Edward Drinker Cope and Charles Othniel Marsh. The two scientists began as friends, but they soon became bitter enemies.

In the late nineteenth century, it became apparent that sites in states such as Colorado, Nebraska and Wyoming were extremely rich in fossils. Cope and Marsh competed against each other to see who could uncover the most new species.

Out in the field, their teams resorted to hurling rocks at each other and destroying bones so their rivals wouldn't get them. Cope and Marsh insulted each other in print and obsessively pointed out each other's mistakes. When Cope reconstructed the skeleton of a marine reptile with a long neck and a short tail called the Elasmosaurus, he mistakenly placed its skull on its tail. Marsh did his best to draw attention to Cope's error and damage his reputation.

Despite their underhand tactics, the two men increased the number of known dinosaur species to almost 150, and their discoveries included such well-known dinosaurs as Stegosaurus, Diplodocus and Triceratops.

Although they were sometimes very eccentric characters, the great fossil hunters of the nineteenth century changed the way we think about our world. The extinct creatures they discovered still fascinate us today, as shown by the success of films such as *Jurassic Park*.

How do we know about the dinosaur hunters?

When you examine a recent period of history like the nineteenth century, there can be a huge amount of surviving evidence to consider. Between them the dinosaur hunters left thousands of pages of notes, journals and illustrations. They published papers in scientific journals and their discoveries were written about in newspapers.

Sometimes the evidence is so vast it can be hard to sift through. For example, Edward Drinker Cope wrote over 1,400 scientific papers. He was so determined to identify new species before his great rival Charles Othniel Marsh that he published his findings at an astonishing rate.

Photography was commercially introduced in 1839, and many images of the dinosaur hunters survive. Pictures of Charles Othniel Marsh on digs portray him as a fearless explorer, setting out into dangerous territory to discover new species.

Many of the fossils themselves also survive, and can be viewed in natural history museums around the world.

Timeline

225 million years ago
The first dinosaurs appear, in the
Triassic period.

201 million years ago
The beginning of the Jurassic period, which
sees giant dinosaurs emerge.

145 million years ago
The beginning of the Cretaceous period, which
sees more diversity in dinosaurs. (Most of the
dinosaurs in *Jurassic Park* were from this
period, so it should really have been called
Cretaceous Park.)

65 million years ago
Dinosaurs wiped out. According to the scientist
Luis Alvarez, this was because of a meteorite
impact. The Cenozoic era and the age of
mammals begins. Humans eventually appear,

but they'll have more pressing things than fossil hunting for a while, so watch out for a rather large gap in the timeline...

1796

George Cuvier presents a paper analysing the skeletons of elephants and mammoths, and proves that species can become extinct. This lays the foundation for the dinosaur hunters of the nineteenth century.

1811

Mary Anning finds the skeleton of an Ichthyosaur in Lyme Regis, England.

1822

Gideon Mantell discovers fossilised teeth from a creature he names the 'Iguanodon'.

Timeline

1829

William Buckland publishes a paper on 'coprolites', a term he has coined for fossilised poo.

1831

Gideon Mantell publishes a paper called 'The Age of Reptiles', which describes a time when giant reptiles were the dominant animals. It is later known as the Mesozoic era.

1836

Edward Hitchcock identifies giant fossilised footprints in Connecticut Valley, USA, but concludes they were made by ancient birds.

1841

Richard Owen gives the name 'dinosauria' to a group of land reptiles that have vanished from the Earth. Dinosaurs will go on to capture the imagination of the public.

Timeline

1864

Edward Drinker Cope and Charles Othniel
Marsh meet on friendly terms. They will soon
become bitter enemies and compete to see
who can name and discover the most new
dinosaur species.

1881

The Natural History Museum opens in London.

1902

Barnum Brown finds the partial skeleton of a
huge dinosaur in the Hell Creek formation in
Montana, USA.

1905

Henry Fairfield Osborn names Barnum Brown's
creature Tyrannosaurus rex.

Dinosaur Hunter Hall of Fame

Georges Cuvier (1769-1832)

French naturalist whose work was hugely influential on the fossil hunters of the nineteenth century. He used his expert knowledge of animal anatomy to interpret fossils, and it was said that he could reconstruct an entire skeleton from just a single bone. He proved that species could become extinct, and has been called the 'father of palaeontology'.

William Buckland (1784-1856)

English clergyman with a passion for fossils. He became president of the Geological Society in 1824 and wrote the first full account of what would later be called a dinosaur. Like many early dinosaur hunters, Buckland was a very odd character. His other great interest was eating unusual meat, and his ambition was to scoff every animal in the world.

Dinosaur Hunter Hall of Fame

Gideon Mantell (1790-1852)

English surgeon who gathered an important collection of fossils in the early nineteenth century. But his obsession took its toll. Towards the end of his life, his wife left him and he ended up with huge debts.

Edward Hitchcock (1793-1864)

President of Amherst College in Massachusetts, USA and early geologist. He discovered fossilised tracks that he believed were made by giant ancient birds. We now know they were made by dinosaurs.

Mary Anning (1799-1847)

Fossil collector who lived in Lyme Regis, England. Her findings had a massive impact on how we see the history of life on Earth. As a woman, she was never allowed to join the

Dinosaur Hunter Hall of Fame

Geological Society and be fully accepted by the scientific community. But the true importance of her discoveries is now recognised.

Sir Richard Owen (1804-1892)

Scientist who coined the term 'dinosaur'. He was one of the most ambitious figures in the fossil-hunting world, and was ruthless in his treatment of rivals such as Gideon Mantell.

Thomas Huxley (1825-1895)

English biologist and friend of Charles Darwin. He was a strong supporter of Darwin's theory of evolution by natural selection, which was controversial at the time. Huxley suggested that birds evolved from small carnivorous dinosaurs, an idea that's now accepted.

Dinosaur Hunter Hall of Fame

Othniel Charles Marsh (1831-1899)

Fossil hunter who competed with Edward
Drinker Cope to discover new species in
the west of the USA in the late nineteenth
century. The feud spurred both men on to
great achievement, and between them they
discovered many of the best-known dinosaurs.

Edward Drinker Cope (1840-1897)

Professor of Natural Sciences at Haverford
College in the USA and adversary of Othniel
Charles Marsh in the 'Bone Wars'. He published
over 1,400 papers and discovered over 1,000
new species, including many dinosaurs.

Barnum Brown (1873-1963)

American fossil hunter who made important
discoveries at the end of the Victorian era and

the beginning of the twentieth century. He found several partial skeletons of the huge dinosaur that would become known as the 'Tyrannosaurus rex'.

Luis Alvarez (1911-1988)

Although he was a physicist and not a palaeontologist, Alvarez came up with a very famous theory about dinosaurs in 1980. He proposed that dinosaurs became extinct when the Earth was struck by a meteorite 65 million years ago.

Michael Crichton (1942-2008)

American author and screenwriter who wrote the novel *Jurassic Park*, in which dinosaurs are brought back to life. In 1993, Steven Spielberg adapted it into a blockbuster film that inspired a new generation to take an interest in fossils.

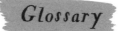

Glossary

Antilles
A chain of islands in the West Indies, including Jamaica, Cuba and Puerto Rico.

Biped
A creature that uses two legs for walking, such as a human or Tyrannosaurus rex.

Bone bed
A layer of rock containing a dense collection of fossilised remains.

Carnivore
A meat-eater. By contrast, herbivores ate only plants.

Coprolite
A piece of fossilised poo. We can learn about the diet of extinct creatures from it.

Cretaceous
The last period of the Mesozoic era.

Extinct
A species with no living members is called extinct. The idea that a species could die out altogether was not widely accepted until the nineteenth century.

Femur
The upper bone in the back limb of a dinosaur. In humans, the femur is the thigh bone.

Field work
Practical work carried out in a natural environment rather than a laboratory.

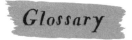

Glossary

Fossil
The preserved remains or traces of prehistoric plants and animals.

Frill
A sheet of bone extending from the back of the skull in dinosaurs such as Triceratops.

Geology
The study of the history of the Earth, especially through rocks.

Ghost town
A town which has been completely abandoned. For example, a town could have been built around a mine that has run out.

Jurassic
The middle period of the Mesozoic era.

Mesozoic
The era in which the dinosaurs lived. It is divided into the Triassic, Jurassic and Cretaceous periods.

Naturalist
Someone who studies plants and animals. Not to be confused with naturists, who don't wear any clothes.

New World
A name for North and South America that was coined when they were first 'discovered' and explored by Europeans in the early sixteenth century.

Nickel
A small coin used in the USA that's worth five cents.

Glossary

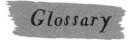

Palaeontology
The study of ancient
life, especially
through plant and
animal fossils.

Quadruped
A creature that
uses four legs for
walking, such as a cat
or Triceratops.

Triassic
The first period of the
Mesozoic era.

Vertebrae
In dinosaur skeletons,
these are small bones
that fit together to
form the neck, back
and tail.

THE LONG-LOST
SECRET DIARY OF THE
WORLD'S WORST

Shortlisted for the
Lancashire School Library Service
Fantastic Book Awards (FBA) 2017–18.

*'Although easy to read, the vocabulary is
great and the plot lines engaging – excellent
reads for developing readers.'*
Library Girl and Book Boy Blog

THE LONG-LOST SECRET DIARY OF THE WORLD'S WORST DINOSAUR HUNTER

Illustrated by Sarah Horne

PB ISBN: 978-1-912233-19-9

THE LONG-LOST SECRET DIARY OF THE WORLD'S WORST ASTRONAUT

Written by Tim Collins Illustrated by Sarah Horne

PB ISBN: 978-1-912233-20-5

THE LONG-LOST SECRET DIARY OF THE WORLD'S WORST KNIGHT

Written by Tim Collins Illustrated by Sarah Horne

PB ISBN: 978-1-912006-67-0

THE LONG-LOST SECRET DIARY OF THE WORLD'S WORST PIRATE

Written by Tim Collins Illustrated by Sarah Horne

PB ISBN: 978-1-912006-66-3

A selected list of Scribo titles

The prices shown below are correct at the time of going to press. However, The Salariya Book Company reserves the right to show new retail prices on covers, which may differ from those previously advertised.

Gladiator School by Dan Scott

1	Blood Oath	978-1-908177-48-3	£6.99
2	Blood & Fire	978-1-908973-60-3	£6.99
3	Blood & Sand	978-1-909645-16-5	£6.99
4	Blood Vengeance	978-1-909645-62-2	£6.99
5	Blood & Thunder	978-1-910184-20-2	£6.99
6	Blood Justice	978-1-910184-43-1	£6.99

Iron Sky by Alex Woolf

| 1 | Dread Eagle | 978-1-909645-00-4 | £9.99 |
| 2 | Call of the Phoenix | 978-1-910184-87-5 | £6.99 |

Children of the Nile by Alain Surget

1	Cleopatra must be Saved!	978-1-907184-73-4	£5.99
2	Caesar, Who's he?	978-1-907184-74-1	£5.99
3	Prisoners in the Pyramid	978-1-909645-59-2	£5.99
4	Danger at the Circus!	978-1-909645-60-8	£5.99

Ballet School by Fiona Macdonald

1. Peter & The Wolf	978-1-911242-37-6	£6.99
2. Samira's Garden	978-1-912006-62-5	£6.99

Aldo Moon by Alex Woolf

1 Aldo Moon and the Ghost at Gravewood Hall	978-1-908177-84-1	£6.99

The Shakespeare Plot by Alex Woolf

1 Assassin's Code	978-1-911242-38-3	£9.99
2 The Dark Forest	978-1-912006-95-3	£9.99
3 The Powder Treason	978-1-912006-33-5	£9.99

Visit our website at:

www.salariya.com

All Scribo and Salariya Book Company titles can be ordered from your local bookshop, or by post from:

The Salariya Book Co. Ltd,
25 Marlborough Place
Brighton
BN1 1UB